But mine is quite different,
it's not what you think.

For mine is *not blue*...

My Shadow is PINK

For Colin.

You are loved.
Exactly as you are.

SCOTT StUART

My dad has a shadow
that's blue as can be,
and there's nothing but *blue*
in my whole family tree.

My shadow loves ponies
and books and pink toys,
princesses, fairies, and
things *"not for boys"*.

But there's one thing it likes most I have found...

It loves wearing dresses
and dancing around!

It **spins**...

and it **sparkles**...

and it *twirls* through the air!

Then stops as my Dad walks in with a stare.

it is **JUST** a phase.

Dad's shadow is *blue*, it is *big*, it is *strong*.
But when I stand with it I just feel so wrong.

I wish mine was blue like all of the others,
I wish mine was blue like my Dad's and my brothers.

I'd be part of the group,
of that there's no doubt, but I cannot fit in
when my shadow *stands out!*

Now things are all changing and that is not cool.
I'm ready to start my
first day at school.

YOU'LL NEED:

- pencils
- and books
- and lunch you must bring.

DRESS UP
with your shadow!
(in its favourite thing)

My heart skips a beat as **I put on a dress**
and I look at my Dad who is anxious and stressed.

He takes me to class and I turn to say bye,
His face is all worried, there's
fear in his eyes.

So I step in the doorway and puff out my chest...
One thing is clear... I'm not like the rest.

I try to say *hi* but my voice is too quiet.

The kids turn around
and the room, it goes silent.

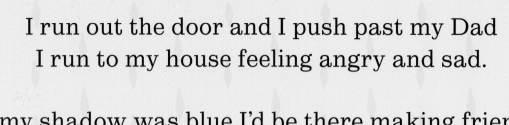

I run out the door and I push past my Dad
I run to my house feeling angry and sad.

If my shadow was blue I'd be there making friends.
I'd be laughing and playing and drawing with pens.

I rip off my dress, throw it down to the floor.
I won't wear it again. **Not ever. No more.**

Just then at my door
came a soft little knock...

It's my Dad walking in
and I look up in shock.

Both he and his shadow
in dresses they stood!

With **shimmering seams**
and *pink sparkling hoods!*

He speaks in a voice that's quite soft but is stern.

Pick up that dress!
You must listen and learn.

Your shadow is pink,
I see now it's true.

It's not just a shadow,
**it's your
inner-most you.**

He showed me the photos of parents and brothers
and sisters and aunts and uncles and others.

"We've all had a shadow that's hidden from eyes.

Sometimes our shadow,
it lives in disguise.

His shadow loves **painting** and **fashion** and **art**.

Her shadow loves **engines** and **powerful cars**.

His shadow loves **dance** with its **turns** and its **twirls**.

Her shadow she hides it,
her shadow likes **girls**.

His shadow loves **theatre**
and **acting** and **plays**.

Her shadow loves **science**
and **planets** and **space**.

Your shadow is **YOU**

and pink it will be,

so stand up with your shadow and yell

THIS IS ME!

And some they will love you...
and some they will not.

But those that do love you
they'll love you a lot.

So put on that dress,
and get back to school,
if someone won't like you then
THEY are the fool.

My heart nearly burst
and my shadow *it soared!*

I picked up the dress
and wore it once more.

We ran out the door,
this time holding hands.

My Dad and our shadows,
together we stand.

I stride in my class and I puff out my chest,
I may be different, but *different is best.*

I join a small group, though in I don't blend,
they look up and smile.

Will you be our friend?

SCOTT StUART

Scott has, for as long as he can remember, been in love with the art of storytelling.
He lives in Melbourne, Australia with his wife & son and loves to write stories that empower kids.

Check out Scott's other books at
scottstuart.co

Larrikin House

An imprint of Learning Discovery Pty Ltd
142-144 Frankston Dandenong Rd, Dandenong South Victoria 3175 Australia

www.larrikinhouse.com

First Published in Australia by Larrikin House 2020 (larrikinhouse.com)

Written by: Scott Stuart
Illustrated by: Scott Stuart
Cover Designed by: Scott Stuart
Artwork by: Mary Anastasiou (imaginecreative.com.au)

A CIP catalogue record for this book is available from the National Library of Australia. http://catalogue.nla.gov.au

ISBN: 9780648728757 (Hardback)
ISBN: 9780648728764 (Paperback)

FOREST FRIENDLY
This book is printed on paper sourced
from sustainable forests

NATIONAL
LIBRARY
OF AUSTRALIA

A catalogue record for this
book is available from the
National Library of Australia